tiger tales
5 River Road, Suite 128, Wilton, CT 06897
Published in the United States 2015
Originally published in Great Britain 2015
by Little Tiger Press
Text copyright © 2015 Steve Smallman
Illustrations copyright © 2015 Ada Grey
ISBN-13: 978-1-58925-171-7
ISBN-10: 1-58925-171-7
Printed in China
LTP/1400/0989/0914

For more insight and activities,
visit us at www.tigertalesbooks.com

For Gabriella, who makes the BEST animal noises EVER! – S. S.

To GavGav, POOP, PARP, PHWEEP! – A.G.

Hiccupotamus

by STEVE SMALLMAN

Illustrated by ADA GREY

tiger tales

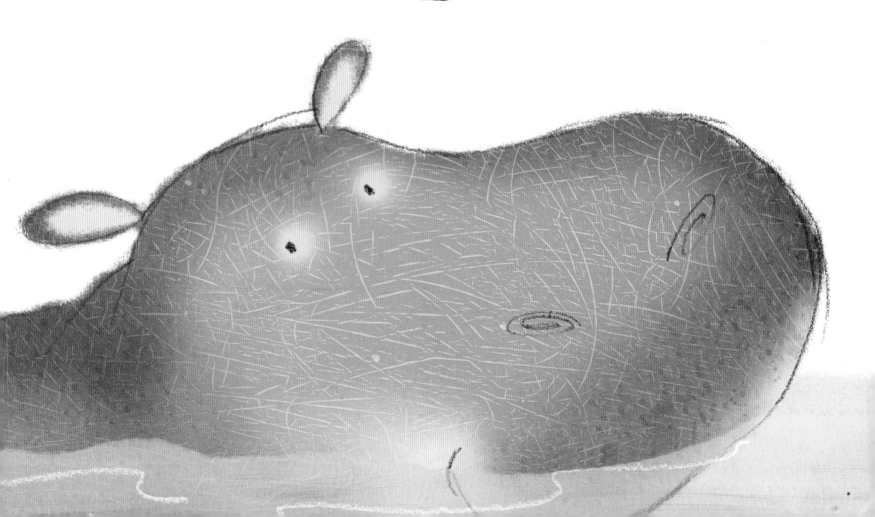

A mouse sat down by a bubbling creek—
The creek went **bubble** and
the mouse went squeak!

Squeak, squeak, bubble, bubble,
squeak, squeak, squeak.
Squeak, squeak,
bubble, **bubble**,
squeak, squeak,
squeak!

A little bird tweeted,
"What a
GREAT song!
And if you don't
mind, I'll sing along!"

"Wait!" cried Centipede. "You need a beat!" So he tapped out a rhythm with his tappity feet ...

Tip-tap-a-tippy-tappy, tweet-tweet-tweet,

Squeak, squeak, bubble, bubble, squeak, Squeak, Squeak!

Monkey heard the music and he cried, "Woo-hoo! That sounds so cool. Can I join in, too?"

Warthog said,
"I'VE GOT A MUSICAL TUM!"
Then he banged on his belly like a big bass drum ...

tweet-tweet-tweet,

Squeak, squeak,
bubble, bubble,
squeak, squeak,
squeak!

Then
along came a

great
BIG

croc

odile.

He listened to the music and it made him smile!
He reached in his pocket and he took out a bone...

Then he played on his teeth like a xylophone!

PLINK PLINK PLINK-A-PLONK! PLINKETTY-PLOO!

BOOM-BA-DA-BOOM-BOOM!
Ooh, ooh, ooh!
Tip-tap-a-tippy-tappy,
tweet-tweet-tweet.
Squeak, squeak, bubble, bubble,
squeak, squeak,
squeak!

They danced and they played 'til a quarter to four,
Then they all flopped down in a heap on the floor.
"Wow!" cried Mouse. "Now, wasn't that fun?
You guys totally ROCKED! Well done!"

"Thanks!" they cried. "We all helped, it's true,
But the person we should
thank is..."

"Excuse me?" Mouse said. "But what did you do?
Monkey was the one who went ooh, ooh, ooh!
Centipede **tapped** with his **tappity** feet,
And this little bird went tweet, tweet, tweet."

"Warthog banged on his musical tum—
It went BOOM-BA-DA-BOOM!
like a big bass drum!
Crocodile played plink, plinketty-ploo,

Hippo said,
"I've been drinking fizzy-wizzy pop!
I'm hiccupping bubbles
and I just can't stop!"